FEB 1 4 2017

TIME TWISTERS

HAUNTED TIME

Calico

An Imprint of Magic Wagon
abdopublishing.com

BY KATHRYN LAY ILLUSTRATED BY DAVE BARDIN

J
Lay

$27.07

FOR MICHELLE AND PARKER AND THE FUTURE TIMES YOU WILL HAVE TOGETHER. —KL

FOR MY MOM, WHO GAVE ME MY FIRST SKETCHBOOK AND HAS NEVER STOPPED GIVING. —DB

abdopublishing.com

Published by Magic Wagon, a division of ABDO, PO Box 398166, Minneapolis, Minnesota 55439. Copyright © 2017 by Abdo Consulting Group, Inc. International copyrights reserved in all countries. No part of this book may be reproduced in any form without written permission from the publisher. Calico™ is a trademark and logo of Magic Wagon.

Printed in the United States of America, North Mankato, Minnesota.
102016
012017

**THIS BOOK CONTAINS
RECYCLED MATERIALS**

Written by Kathryn Lay
Illustrated by Dave Bardin
Edited by Tamara L. Britton & Megan M. Gunderson
Designed by Laura Mitchell

Publisher's Cataloging-in-Publication Data

Names: Lay, Kathryn, author. | Bardin, Dave, illustrator.
Title: Haunted time / by Kathryn Lay ; illustrated by Dave Bardin.
Description: Minneapolis, MN : Magic Wagon, 2017. | Series: Time
    twisters ; Book 2
Summary: Luis, Tyler, Casey, and robot cat Steel use Tesla's Time Twister
    to journey to a haunted house, where they face a haunted house and
    continue trying to help Uncle Cyrus, who remains stuck in time.
Identifiers: LCCN 2016947643 | ISBN 9781624021787 (lib. bdg.) |
    ISBN 978162402388 (ebook) | ISBN 9781624022685 (Read-to-me
    ebook)
Subjects: LCSH: Time travel--Juvenile fiction. | Best friends--Juvenile
    fiction. | Adventure and adventurers--Juvenile fiction. | Survival--
    Juvenile fiction.
Classification: DDC [Fic]--dc23
LC record available at http://lccn.loc.gov/2016947643

TABLE
OF
CONTENTS

BACK IN TIME

Luis Sanchez sat on his back porch, knees pulled to his chin. He stared at the large shed in the field just past his backyard.

It seemed like a dream, but just an hour before he had been on a spaceship. He and his best friends, Tyler and Casey Jenson, and Tyler's robot cat, Steel, had snuck into his dad's shed. Tyler and Casey had found a strange-looking key at their dad's house. They had brought it over, sure it would fit the big lock on the shed. They were right.

They knew there was something secret their fathers were working on inside, but they'd never dreamed it was a time machine.

A time machine.

"We were on a real spaceship. We battled aliens and a robot. And I was the captain!" Luis said out loud.

"We sure did," a voice said from behind him. Something tapped him on the head.

Luis yelled and jumped off the porch.

He glared at Tyler, who was doubled over, laughing.

"You should've seen yourself," Tyler said. He grinned and waved his arm, a crutch swinging wildly.

Casey helped Luis stand. "I didn't think someone who loved adventure as much as you would be so jumpy," she said.

Luis shrugged. "I was thinking about Tesla's Time Twister. And what Dad was going to say when . . . if . . . I tell him about what we did."

Steel rolled over to Luis and sat by his foot. Luis bent down and rubbed the head of the cold, metal robot cat.

Casey said, "If we tell our dads, we'll be grounded for a really long time. For all time!"

"Look!" Tyler shouted.

Luis turned around. Past the backyard fence, the shed seemed to glow. A loud hum came from within.

"What's going on?" Casey asked.

"It's the Time Twister," Luis said, his voice coming out in a squeak. "Someone turned it on."

Tyler shook his head. "But . . . there's no one in there. We locked it when we left. And your dad isn't home."

Luis swallowed hard. What if they had messed up the machine and it was going to explode or pull the whole neighborhood into some other time?

He started across the yard toward the shed.

"Are you nuts?" Casey asked. She ran after him, her jacket full of tools and gadgets clinking as she went.

"I have to check it out," Luis said. "We're the ones who got it going again. What if something bad is happening?"

Tyler moved past them, his metal crutches glinting in the sun. "Maybe I can fix it. I'm the one who wants to be an astronaut someday. I know the most about robots and machines."

Luis was gasping for air when they got to the shed door. He pulled the strange tree-shaped key from his pocket. He unlocked the huge lock. As before, it set off sparks before it opened.

He opened the door slowly.

At the back of the building, on a wooden platform, Tesla's Time Twister shimmered with a white glow.

"We forgot to put the tarp back over it," Casey said. "Our dads will know for sure someone was in here."

Luis walked toward the machine. "They'll also know when they see it glowing. We have to

figure out what's going on. Come on, step inside so we can close the door."

MEEOOW! BOING!

Steel rolled across the floor and stopped beside Luis.

Its eyes flashed red. Then a voice drifted from its speakers.

"Luis, I need your help!"

Luis knelt down beside Steel.

"Uncle Cyrus? I didn't think we could hear you through Steel anymore after we came back," Luis said.

Casey and Tyler ran across the shed. "Is that your uncle Cyrus?"

Luis nodded. "Yeah, I thought we'd lost him in time."

Cyrus spoke. "It seems that because you activated Tesla's Time Twister and I learned how to communicate through this robot feline, I can now do so whenever it is near the machine.

I have even found that I can turn on the Time Twister, though I cannot control my body, which is tied into the pull of the machine."

Luis walked up the steps. He entered the code, 10, 10, 10, on the machine. The door opened and he went inside. Casey and Tyler followed him. Casey held Steel in her arms.

"You said that you need our help," Luis said. He sat down in one of the chairs.

Casey placed Steel on the floor.

"After we parted, I found myself inside another story," Cyrus said. "It is different from all the years of watching time go past. I feel there is something I must do. Yet, I am not able to participate in the story."

Tyler said, "Maybe that means you can come back to real time somehow."

Steel's eyes blinked on and off. Luis wondered if his uncle was gaining more control of Tyler's cat as time passed.

"I have wondered the same. I am also afraid that without your help I will be trapped in the place I find myself now," Uncle Cyrus said.

Casey folded her arms. "Hey, I feel sorry for your uncle, but we *just* got back! Last time you were nearly smashed by a giant robot and lizard aliens tried to capture us."

"Yeah, but we were there to stop it," Luis said.

He whirled around as the door to the Time Twister closed with a whoosh. Lights around them blinked and glowed.

"Uh, what's going on, Uncle Cyrus?" Luis asked.

"I'm sorry, but I need your help now," his uncle said. "You and your friends should sit down. I am resetting the dates for time travel."

Casey and Tyler hurried to two of the seats.

"What does he think he's doing?" Casey shouted.

Luis's heart pounded. They were off to another adventure. He was both excited and scared. He looked at the set of dates near his chair. They began to spin.

Backward.

When they stopped, the date read: July 17, 1994.

Steel let out a loud *MEEOW-BOING!*

Luis's stomach squeezed as everything twisted and turned. He felt as if he were spinning in a tornado again. The lights in the Time Twister flickered and went dark.

Luis tried to yell but made no sound as he twisted through time. He squeezed his eyes shut and wondered what he would see when he opened them.

The air around him was suddenly warm. He felt a breeze and heard birds singing.

"Hey, Luis, are you going to talk into the camera or fall asleep?" a voice asked.

Luis opened his eyes. He looked around and saw that he was standing on grass. Tyler and Casey were beside him. Steel was on the ground in front of Tyler. They hadn't lost him this time.

"Come on, remember how we rehearsed it?" the voice asked.

Luis blinked. In front of him were two men and a woman. They were holding old-fashioned movie cameras and microphones on long poles. One man knelt on the grass beside a group of boxes, going through them and pulling out strange-looking gadgets.

Casey whispered, "Ooh, are we movie stars?"

The woman smiled. "Casey, dear, I wouldn't count on it. Although, if we can do this right and stop or send back the ghosts this time, you'll be a lot richer and a little more famous."

Luis's mouth fell open. "Did you say ghosts?"

The man behind the camera leaned away from it. "What do you think we're looking for in

New York's famous Serling Mansion? Penguins? Of course we're looking for ghosts."

He jerked his head as if to point behind Luis.

Luis and his friends turned. They stood in front of a three-story wood house. Its windows looked like eyes. Paint peeled away from old boards that had once been green.

Luis stared at the closed door. It had a dragon-shaped knocker.

While he watched, the door slowly swung open. Air that smelled old and musty drifted out of the house.

Luis shook his head and shuddered. "I'm not going in there."

He took a step away from the old house. It looked like part of a scary movie.

But, it also looked like adventure.

"What are we supposed to do?" Luis asked.

The cameraman walked over to stand beside Luis. He put a hand on Luis's shoulder.

"Welcome to the Serling Mansion. We're supposed to clean anything otherworldly or ghostly out of here. I did a lot of research before accepting this job. Sorry, but you three are not known for your fact-finding. And apparently you're not known for your memory, either."

Luis's throat felt dry. His palms were wet.

"Uh, we're not?" he asked.

The cameraman said, "I'm Bob. The one you spoke to on the phone." He pointed to the house. "This place is full of history and legend. There have been lots of accidents, strange noises, and ghost sightings. It was a gangster hideout, and treasure hunters have checked it out. I even read that the famous scientist Nikola Tesla lived here for a brief time. Back in the mid-1920s."

Tyler raised his eyebrows at his friends. "So, what are we doing exactly?" Tyler asked.

The man grinned. "You are the Haunting Exterminators of course. Ghost hunters. And

Simsbury Public Library
Children's Room

we're here to film the three of you facing whatever haunts this house."

Casey asked, "And what do we do after we find it?"

Bob frowned. "Get rid of it, of course. That is, if the ghost doesn't take us all. The last team that tried this about five years ago . . . well, let's just say that no one knows where they are to this day."

THE HAUNTED HOUSE

Luis backed away from the house. "What do you mean, whatever haunts this house? Don't you know?"

The woman said, "Ghosts, phantoms, poltergeists . . . whatever is inside. Like Bob said, they say that there were some college guys trying to ghost hunt that went in and never came out again."

Then she yelled to the man going through the boxes. "Isn't that right, Parker? Those guys disappeared."

Parker stood and stretched. "That's what they say, Darla. Course, it could've been a college prank. The stories say that the police and the boys' families searched inside but couldn't find them. They said there were strange noises and they saw things moving out of the corners of their eyes."

Tyler turned and said, "Your uncle didn't say anything about ghosts and haunted houses and people who were gobbled up inside them."

Luis pointed at the house. "Uncle Cyrus was . . . is . . . a scientist. So are you two. I'm the one who reads adventure books and watches scary movies. If anyone should be scared, it's me. But I trust Uncle Cyrus. He brought us here for a reason. There's something here that can help him."

Bob said, "I don't know about this Cyrus guy, but this place has been boarded up for years. We just pulled off the boards and unlocked the door a few minutes ago."

Darla set the microphone on the ground. "Bob's right. You hired me and him and Parker to film this and do it right. You messed up when you faked that last haunting. This is your chance to repair your reputation. And to make us famous."

Luis said, "Come on, Casey, Tyler. For Uncle Cyrus. And the adventure." He pointed at the equipment on the ground. "And for new gadgets, Casey."

Casey gasped. She ran over to check out the strange objects. "Are these for finding ghosts?"

Bob nodded. "They're supposed to be, but they haven't worked yet. And for measuring ectoplasm and recording voices from beyond."

"Okay, let's go," Casey said. She grabbed one of the cases and marched across the grass and up to the porch. She climbed the brick steps and peered into the darkness behind the open door.

Luis shrugged his shoulders, grabbed Steel, and said, "Come on, Tyler."

The camera crew followed behind them.

"Darla," Bob shouted. "Look at that cat!"

The sound woman walked beside Luis. "Unusual cat you have there. Is it some kind of fancy toy?"

Luis shook his head. "It's a robot. Tyler built it himself."

Darla touched Steel's head. Its whiskers spun around.

MEOWWZ-BOING!

"Strange," Darla said.

From inside, Luis heard a sound. It seemed far away, but it sounded like a sigh.

"What was that?" Tyler asked.

Luis took a deep breath. "The wind. Just the wind."

"You go first," Casey said. "It was your uncle who brought us here."

Luis couldn't argue with that. Instead, he put one foot into the house. The floor creaked. Why did floors always creak in haunted house movies?

"This isn't a movie," he mumbled.

Luis walked into the house. The moment he did, cold air rushed past him. He whirled around.

"Come on in," he said. He reached for a light switch, but when he flipped it, nothing happened.

"Hey, where are the lights?" Casey asked.

Bob stepped inside and sniffed. "Musty." He pulled several flashlights from a bag. "Everyone gets one of these. We had them turn the electricity back on, but the owner said nothing is working right. Even the plumbing only works a little bit."

Luis turned on his flashlight and shone it around the room. There were a few pieces of furniture, all covered in dirty white cloths and cobwebs. An old clock hung on one wall. The hands were broken off, lying on the floor below. A wooden staircase curved to the floor above.

Casey moved the beam of her flashlight up the stairs.

"I bet those creak, too," Luis said.

The camera crew began unpacking the cases. Bob shook out one of the furniture covers and placed it neatly on the floor. They put the strange-looking instruments on the cloth.

"These are really cool," Casey said. She picked up each one, turned it over and around, touched switches and gears, and asked what they were called.

"That's a laser grid. That one's a footstep tracker. We can set those up if we stay the night. The one next to it is my Cold Spot Environment Detector," Parker said. "You act as if you've never used them before. None of them have ever worked for us, but we keep hoping, right?"

Tyler wiped cobwebs away with one of his crutches. "So, we've never found a ghost? Wouldn't that mean we're fakes?"

Bob looked up from a large camera. "Fakes? Fakes just pretend. We're really trying to find something. But we have to find something this time, or we're out of business."

From above them came a loud scraping sound.

Luis looked up. He put Steel on the floor and whispered, "Is that you, Uncle Cyrus?"

There was only silence from the cat.

"You call your robot Uncle Cyrus?" Darla asked.

Luis nodded. "He also answers to Steel."

Something crashed upstairs. Tyler moved toward the staircase. "That sounded like glass. There's something up there. Or the wind inside is really strong."

"Everyone grab an instrument," Luis said. If he was in charge, he wanted to get this adventure moving. Where was his uncle Cyrus? Were there really ghosts? Had they captured his uncle?

"Don't forget Steel," Tyler said.

Luis grabbed the cat and shone his flashlight on the steps. He led the group up the stairs. He didn't hear any other noises, but the higher he climbed, the colder it felt.

He had read books and seen movies where they talked about a "cold spot" in a haunted house, but this whole mansion felt weirdly cold. Luis shivered.

At the top of the stairs, he saw a long, narrow hallway. There were doors on either side. They were all closed, and he didn't see any kind of furniture in the hall. There was a large window near the stairs.

"This window is broken," Luis said.

Tyler and Casey stood beside the window. They could see out into the yard and the street. Everything was quiet. Everything looked like a normal neighborhood.

"I guess a big gust of wind broke it, right?" Bob said. "Or maybe someone threw a ball at it. I'm sure an abandoned house is a target for anyone goofing off."

Casey bent down to look at the floor near the window. She studied the broken window, then looked back down at the ground. "No, nothing came through that window from outside. The window was broken from the inside."

Bob's eyes went wide. "From the inside?"

Casey nodded. "Yes, there is very little glass inside. Most of it is outside on the ground, beneath the window."

Luis leaned out and looked at the glass below. "So, someone did this from inside?"

Parker shrugged. "Or some *thing*."

They walked down the hall, holding out light and sound instruments.

Luis walked beside Bob.

"This house has been here for ninety years, since 1904. It's had twelve different owners. No one has stayed long," Bob said.

Luis was glad that he and his friends weren't alone. But he wondered if that was why they hadn't heard from Uncle Cyrus yet.

Luis had to find a way that he and his friends and Steel could separate from the others, just for a few minutes.

Tyler pointed down the hall. "There's an open door down there."

Luis had seen it too. He stopped. "Should we go inside?"

"That's why we're here," Darla said. She waved the thermal video camera around and held her microphone in front of her.

Tyler nudged Luis. He looked around and whispered, "I'm not comfortable with this place. There aren't any robots to fiddle with except for Steel. Everything is old and backward. Did you see those silly machines?"

Luis whispered back, "We've got to talk to Uncle Cyrus. Let's get those three in that room first. Then we'll try to contact Cyrus while we're in the hall."

Casey agreed to the plan. "Hey, can you three go into the room and see what your machines read? We'll stay right outside the door and see if any ghosts try to contact us."

Luis was surprised when the others agreed. They walked into the room, slowly at first. As they walked around, the lights from the camera and their flashlights brightened the dark room.

Luis bent toward Steel. "Uncle Cyrus, please answer me."

Steel's eyes flickered. "I am trying, Luis. But there is interference with my ability to contact you through the cat. Something in this house."

"Is it a ghost?" Casey asked.

The voice from Steel's speakers was silent a moment. "As a scientist, I should say no. But, I can hear voices. They argue and threaten anyone coming into this house."

"Come in here quick!" Bob shouted.

"Hold on!" Luis shouted back.

"Do the voices talk to you?" Tyler asked.

"No," Cyrus said, "only to one another. But they are angry and say that they will destroy this house to get what they want."

Luis's heart pounded. He had to get more information before they joined the others.

He turned away from Steel. Was his uncle hiding information? If he wasn't, why did he think that if he brought Luis and his friends here, they could help him get back to his own time?

He turned back to say something to Cyrus, but Steel was gone.

"Hey, where's Steel?" he asked.

Tyler shrugged. "He was just here."

Luis looked down the hall, but he didn't see the cat. He listened for Steel's rolling feet, but he didn't hear the cat.

In fact, he didn't hear anything. There were no sounds coming from the room. Bob had even stopped yelling at them to come inside.

Luis said, "Something is wrong. It's too quiet."

Tyler and Casey followed him into the room.

It was dark and quiet. He moved his flashlight around the small, empty space.

"Hey, where is everyone? What did you want us to see?" Luis asked.

"I think it was that," Tyler said. He shone his flashlight on the wall, moving it along slowly. There were words, written in shaky black lettering. The skin on Luis's arms was filled with goose bumps as Tyler read the words out loud.

LEAVE OR BE TRAPPED FOREVER!

Through the Wall

Luis stared at the words on the wall. Tyler walked across the room and touched the lettering. "It's slimy. It feels like oil or something."

Casey turned in a circle, shining her flashlight up and down.

"Where did they go? The only way in or out is the door. There isn't even a window in here," she said.

Luis aimed his flashlight down one of the walls. There was something on the floor, in the far corner. He walked across the room and picked it up. It was Bob's thermal video camera, tipped to one side but unharmed.

"Bob wouldn't have left this behind on purpose," Luis said.

Casey took the camera and pushed a button. "This should rewind it. It shows eight minutes of filming, about the time since we walked in the front door."

She held the camera out so they could all see the screen. Luis watched as the video scanned around the front room downstairs, then panned the stairs and showed them moving up. He could see himself leading everyone. Next it showed the broken window, the glass below it, and then the hallway as they walked toward the rooms.

"Look, they're going into the room," Tyler said. He leaned forward.

Luis nudged him. "Move, I can't see."

The video showed Darla moving her EMF meter up and down. Her other hand pressed an earphone against her ear. Parker walked around the room with the Cold Spot Environment Detector.

Luis held his breath.

Suddenly Bob whirled the camera around. There was no sound. Luis wished he could hear what everyone was saying. But what he saw made his stomach lurch. The writing just appeared on the wall. One letter at a time.

Then the camera fell to the floor, the video now recording sideways. The corner of the wall opened and all three people were pulled through it. The opening closed, and the camera showed nothing but a normal-looking wall.

"Did you see that? Something pulled them through the wall!" Tyler said.

Casey pointed to the corner where Luis had found the camera. "Yeah, and something opened the wall first."

Luis ran to the wall and started pounding on it. "I can't find any way to open it from here. We've got to get inside. Did you see what was beside that last set of feet going into the wall?"

Tyler shook his head.

"Steel!" Luis said. "That's what I saw on the edge of the film just before the wall closed. It was Steel's tail, whirling as it disappeared into the wall."

Tyler groaned. "We have to find Steel."

Casey shook the camera. "Stupid thing. Why doesn't it have sound?"

Tyler said, "Come on, we've got to check all the rooms. We need to find Steel so we can find out what Uncle Cyrus knows."

Luis pointed at the wall with the threatening words on them. "Someone or *something* doesn't want us here."

Tyler said, "I know, but we can't leave the crew behind. Or Steel."

Casey led them into the hall. "Where do we start? I count four other doors."

Luis said, "Let's try the rooms on either side of this one first. Maybe there's a button or a lever that opens the secret door in the wall."

Luis went into the room on the left. Inside there was a chest in the middle of the room. He walked over to it and tried to open it, but it was locked.

"Figures," he said.

Tyler walked around the room, hitting a crutch against the walls.

Casey shone her flashlight around the walls, along the window frame, and across the floor. "I don't see anything that might be a way to open a secret door."

They went down the hall to the door on the other side of the mysterious room.

Luis turned the knob, but the door wouldn't open. "I think it's stuck." He took a step back, then shoved his shoulder against the door.

"Ouch!" he shouted.

"Ouch!" came a voice from inside the room.

"There's someone inside," Casey said. She pounded on the door. "Hey! Let us in!"

Tyler put a finger to his lips. "Shh. Maybe there's something in there we don't *want* to let us inside."

Again, Luis threw his weight against the door. With a shudder, it burst open.

Light streamed in through three large windows.

"Whoa!" Tyler shouted.

"Whoa!" his voice echoed.

They searched the room and found nothing.

"We've got two more rooms to check," Casey said, ready to move on. Tyler followed her out the door.

Luis took a step, but a burst of cold air made his teeth chatter. Frost suddenly covered the windows. Luis could see his breath. It was spring outside, but it felt like winter in that room.

"Luis," a voice said.

Luis jumped. He shone his flashlight into the dark corners.

Luis's voice trembled. "Who's there?"

Something touched his shoulder and he ran for the door.

"Hey," Casey shouted when he bumped into her in the hall. "Where's the fire?"

Luis paused just outside the door, rubbing his cold hands together. "No fire, just a ghost calling me by name."

Tyler and Casey stared at him, their eyes growing wide.

"It said your name?" Tyler asked. "Did it say anything else?"

Luis walked away from the room. "No, but something touched me. I'm not going back in there."

He wasn't sure he wanted to go into the other two rooms either, but he didn't want to stay in this house forever. Being scared in his living room watching a movie was one thing. This was too real.

Luis took a deep breath. "I'm not afraid. I can't be," he said. "I'm going to help Uncle Cyrus and get us back home."

Casey nodded.

"And find my cat," Tyler added.

They searched the last two rooms. They didn't find anything except for lots of cobwebs and some dusty furniture. There were no levers, buttons, or secret entrances beyond the walls.

They gathered in the hallway again.

"Great. What do we do now?" Tyler asked. "Three people disappeared. We could be next."

Casey turned on the camera and filmed Luis. "I hope they're okay. We've got to help them too. We're the ones who let them go in that room alone first."

Luis agreed. He didn't believe in haunted houses. Not really. But he decided that this one was too strange to not be haunted. And if it was a ghost, how did it know his name?

Casey said, "Why are there some rooms without windows? That's just weird. And there is only one window at the end of the hall, but it's not as dark in here."

Luis didn't know what to say. The rooms that were so dark felt different. The whole house was cold. But they felt colder and creepier.

"So, where do we look next?" Tyler asked.

From above them came a shout. Then banging. Then the ceiling seemed to shake.

Luis looked up. There was one place they still hadn't looked.

"The attic. The next place we look is the attic," Casey said. "And whatever's up there is trying to scare us into leaving."

Luis shivered. "It's starting to work. This is way scarier than the giant robot and the lizard aliens. At least we could see them."

Footsteps moved across the ceiling. Luis walked to the end of the hall, following the sound above them. He looked up. There was a rope hanging from the ceiling.

"That has to be the attic door," he said. He stood on his tiptoes and stretched his arm as far as he could, but he couldn't reach the loop in the string.

Tyler hurried down the hall. "Let me," he said. He pulled his hand from one of his crutches and raised it above his head. It wobbled and Luis said, "Lean on me."

He held onto Tyler's arm. Together, they pushed the crutch into the air. The handgrip slipped into the plastic ring.

"Now!" Tyler said.

They pulled together and the door opened. Tyler stepped back as a ladder slid toward them. Luis grabbed it and pulled it to the floor. They looked up into the hole above them.

Casey leaned against the ladder. "Climbing up to the attic isn't creepy at all . . ." she said.

Luis said, "You can do it. I'll go first. Tyler can lean against me and you can help him from behind."

Luis grabbed the sides of the ladder and put a foot on the first step.

"Here we go," he said. He began climbing just as a loud wailing drifted from the attic.

WHO IS THOMAS?

By the time Luis reached the top of the ladder, the wailing sound had stopped.

He stepped into the attic and pulled his flashlight from his pocket. The narrow beam did little to light the dark room, but he could tell the room was big.

He bent down and grabbed Tyler's arm. His friend was shaking.

"Maybe you shouldn't have come up here," Luis said. "Me and Casey could've looked around."

Tyler scooted across the floor away from the ladder. He shook his head once he caught his breath. "No way. Staying down there by myself would have been worse!"

Casey stepped into the attic. "I've seen you climb worse than this," she said to her brother. She tugged at her jacket. It clinked and clanked.

"Quiet," Tyler said.

They shone the lights around the room. Casey's beam landed on an old lantern sitting on a small table.

"I found more light," she said. She picked up the lantern and shook it a bit. "There's oil inside." A box of matches lay beside the lantern.

Luis said, "Great. Can you light it?"

"I can take apart a radio and put it together without instructions," Casey said. "I think I can figure out an oil lamp." She turned a knob to raise the wick, took off the glass top, and lit a match. In a moment the lantern was glowing. She held it up and the room was brighter.

"Wow, this isn't just a room. It looks like it goes half the length of the house," Tyler said. "It's more like a whole third floor."

Luis said, "We'd better get moving then."

Tyler called, "Steel! Where are you, Steel?"

Luis yelled, "Uncle Cyrus, can you hear me?"

Casey gave them a little shove. "If they can't, every ghost in here can."

They walked out of the wide room and found a narrow hallway. Luis had never been in an attic, but he didn't think they usually had halls.

Casey had the lantern in one hand and the video camera around her neck. She stopped, put the lantern on the floor, and held up the camera.

"I still think this thing must have sound," Casey said.

Luis knew she never gave up on trying to figure out how to fix any gadget. He watched as she held it to her ear and shook it.

"I was right. Something happened when it was dropped," Casey said. "I can hear rattling."

She unsnapped a pocket in her jacket and pulled out a plastic box. Inside were screwdrivers of all shapes and sizes. She pushed them around, then grabbed one with a blue handle.

After a moment, she had unscrewed the back of the camera. She found some tweezers in another pocket and got to work.

"Aha!" She pulled out a small screw. "Hold this," she said, giving the camera to Luis.

Pulling out a magnifying glass, she looked into the back of the camera and put the little screw into an empty hole. In seconds, she had tightened it and closed the camera.

"Try it," Tyler said. "If it was a robot, I'd just program it to tell us what happened."

Casey turned on the camera and they watched again as Bob swung the camera around the room. They could hear the others talking. Darla was talking about a strong cold spot by the same wall that opened moments later.

"Look! Over there!" Parker said. "Words are appearing on the wall!"

The camera swung to the dark words they had seen. Then there was more talking.

"Wait, stop the video," Luis said. "Go back and replay that."

He listened to the yelling. "Turn it louder." He listened and said, "That's Uncle Cyrus's voice. What is he saying?"

Tyler leaned closer to the camera. "He said, 'We are captured. Dangerous men. Thomas is with us. Ask him for help.'"

The video ended. Luis said, "What men? And who is Thomas?"

Luis frowned. If there were men that had captured them, then maybe it wasn't a haunted house after all. He had been afraid but also excited at the idea of seeing ghosts.

Casey said, "We've got to find Steel and the crew."

Luis turned and walked along the hall. Even if it wasn't ghosts, something bad was going on in the house. Who had captured Bob, Darla, and Parker? Uncle Cyrus had brought Luis and his friends to this time to help him, but they still didn't know how or why.

At the end of the hallway, a sharp turn to the left led to another huge room. They heard voices. Two men were arguing.

Luis put a finger to his lips and pointed.

They inched slowly toward the voices. Luis put a hand out for Casey and Tyler to stop. He peeked around the arched opening.

Luis tried not to make a sound when he saw Bob, Parker, and Darla sitting back to back on the floor. Their hands and feet were bound and handkerchiefs were tied around their mouths.

Two men stood face to face on the other side of the room. One, a man with a beard and mustache, shook his fist at the other.

"What are we going to do with these three? It's another interruption. We've almost run out of places to look for the money and people keep coming here to find ghosts. I bet that old man was lying about the money. Those gangsters didn't hide it here after all."

The other man, much shorter and wearing a bright Hawaiian shirt, shoved his partner's fist away. "It's here somewhere. I just know it. We need more time."

Luis backed away from the door and walked quietly past his friends. He continued back around the corner and motioned for them to follow.

"What's going on?" Casey asked.

"There are two men. They're looking for some kind of money that was hidden here," Luis said.

"I guess they were scaring people away by making the house seem haunted," Tyler said. "Did you see Steel in there?"

Luis shook his head.

Tyler said, "I hope they didn't toss my robot out a window or smash it or something."

"We need to get the police," Casey said.

Tyler pulled out his phone. "Nothing."

Casey laughed. "Are you kidding? You expect a cell phone from the future to work here?"

"Oh, yeah," Tyler said, laughing.

Luis leaned against the wall. It was dangerous to stay there, but he was afraid that they'd never get back home without Uncle Cyrus.

"I wonder who this Thomas guy is?" Luis said out loud.

The air around them got cold. Fast. He looked at Tyler. His teeth chattered. Casey pulled her coat closer around her.

"What's going on?" Tyler asked.

Luis breathed and saw a cloud of air again. "I don't think those crooks are doing this. They can't be that good at pretend haunting."

A voice spoke behind them. "Of course the petty thieves aren't haunting you. No one is, because I am here to help."

Luis whirled around. A man stood behind them. He wore an old-fashioned police uniform. He tipped his hat and smiled.

Luis could see right through the policeman. He pointed at him and said, "You . . ."

The man nodded. "My name is Thomas. And I am the ghost of Serling Mansion."

FINDING STEEL

"Eek!" Casey yelled. Then she held up the video camera and said, "Smile!"

"Others have tried such cameras, but have not caught my true image," Thomas said.

Luis didn't know what to say. A real ghost stood smiling in front of him. He wasn't making scary faces, whirling in the air above them, moaning, groaning, or chasing them like in the movies.

"Are you a police officer?" Tyler asked.

Thomas turned and looked at Tyler. He nodded. "I was. And a good one, too. My last job was to capture two gangsters who had hidden in this house. They took the owners hostage after robbing the First National Bank in 1947."

"Wow," Luis said. "Real gangsters?"

"Yes, and dangerous fellows," Thomas said. He moved farther down the hall, away from where the men were holding the camera crew hostage. "I died trying to capture them. They escaped but were later found and jailed. Legend has it they hid their money from the bank robbery somewhere in this house."

Casey folded her arms. "If they killed you, how do you know all that?"

Thomas smiled. "Smart girl. Because, I was stuck here. There were policemen coming in and out and I heard them talking. And, for many long years I've listened as people who lived in this house came and left. Many come here to talk about the house's history. Others come to search for the money, such as the two men who have your friends. Scoundrels!"

"I guess people moved out because you haunted them?" Luis asked.

"No, I was just here. I can't help it if people feel me or if I scare away some of the ones who come to search for treasure," Thomas said.

Luis pointed down the hall. "Speaking of that, what about those two men in there who captured our friends? They also took an important robot cat we have to find."

"Yes," Thomas said. "I have been watching them all. These men have been here several days. They have torn up many walls. I've tried to scare them away, but their greed keeps them here."

"We have to help our friends escape," Luis said. "Can you help us do that?"

"I have tried to scare them, but perhaps we can try again," Thomas said. "If they leave and your friends are set free, will you all promise to leave here?"

"You bet!" Tyler said. "That is, if we find our cat. It kind of brought us here."

Thomas laughed. "An interesting cat. Yes, I have seen it. I can take you to the strange creature."

The ghost moved quickly down the hall to the large room at the top of the attic steps. He went straight to a far corner of the room and into a wall.

"Hey," Luis said. "Come back!"

He tapped on the wall.

"Hey, that sounds hollow," Tyler said. He put his ear to the wall and called out, "Steel, are you in there?"

There was a muffled sound from behind the wall. Luis couldn't make out any words, but it sounded like Uncle Cyrus.

"We can't hear you. Talk louder!" Luis said.

"I said, yes, the cat and I are in here. The silly thing followed the camera people and the two men grabbed it and stuffed it in here," Uncle Cyrus shouted.

Casey patted pockets in her jacket. She unzipped one at the bottom and pulled out a small hammer.

"I should have guessed you'd have a hammer in that thing," Luis said.

She began tapping the wall. "It comes in handy sometimes."

She tapped along the baseboard until she heard a click. A small opening appeared just above it. The hole was too small to crawl through, but big enough for Luis to reach his arms inside.

"I feel cold metal," Luis said. He pulled until Steel slid from behind the wall.

"Well, it's about time you found us," Uncle Cyrus said.

Steel rolled around the room. Its eyes glowed and its head tilted. Then Thomas appeared. They stared at one another.

"There is someone else here," Thomas said.

"It's my uncle Cyrus," Luis said.

"It's hard for him to show himself, but he's talking through the cat," Casey added.

Thomas faded away, then back again, closer to Steel. "Oh, I see. Your uncle is a ghost?"

Casey pointed the camera at the ghost and Steel. "Not really. He's caught in time. We came here in a time machine that Cyrus and Nikola Tesla built long ago."

The ghost bent closer to the cat. "I have heard of Tesla. One of my teachers had met him. A time machine? That is the cat's meow."

Casey giggled.

"And they say we talk weird," Tyler said.

Luis shrugged.

Voices came from the hallway. Luis whirled around. "Where can we hide? Those men are coming."

Thomas frowned. "I'm sorry, there is no place for you to hide in this part of the house. Only the metal cat can fit in the crawl space."

"Down the stairs, quick!" Casey said. She set the lantern on the floor. It's light spread across the floor around the stairs.

Tyler shook his head. "I can't get back down quickly. You two go on. You'll have to find a way to rescue me, too."

Luis did not want to leave his friend behind. But it wouldn't help if they were all prisoners of the crooks.

He hurried toward the ladder. "Come on, Casey."

"No," she said. "I'm not leaving my brother."

A loud noise echoed around the room. Luis turned to see Thomas moving up and down, screaming and shouting. The screams became wails and his body seemed to glow.

He moved down the hall. Luis watched the glow disappear. Then he heard the screams of the two men.

"Thomas is giving us a chance to get out of the attic. Hurry!" Casey shouted. She started down the ladder and waited for Tyler.

"Here, take Steel," Luis said.

Casey carried the robot cat to the second floor, then came back. Together she and Luis helped Tyler down.

Luis closed the attic door and said, "Come on, we need a place to talk, Uncle Cyrus."

They found the room full of windows and sat beside Steel.

"So, why did you bring us here? Why are you here?" Luis asked.

Cyrus's voice drifted from Steel's speakers. "As you left the spaceship, I was flung back in time to this house. I lost all connection with Tesla's Time Twister. I could see nothing but this time period."

Casey pulled a metal puzzle box from one of her pockets and began to twist and move panels. Luis grinned. When she was concentrating, she liked to keep her hands busy.

"Why did that happen?" Luis asked.

Uncle Cyrus sighed. "Perhaps because you used the Time Twister. I can feel changes in my own access to time. I am thankful that you returned to the Time Twister with your cat. Otherwise, I believe I would be stuck in this time."

Thomas stepped through the wall beside them. "I would welcome the company."

Luis held up his hand. "Great job with those crooks, Thomas."

Thomas looked at Luis's hand. He folded his arms and frowned. "I cannot shake. You would only feel cold. But you are welcome."

They heard footsteps from above, and then a banging noise.

"Those men are looking again for the money," Thomas said. "I have come to believe that if an honest person finds the money, I can leave this house."

"And if he can go, perhaps that will allow me to leave this time as well," Uncle Cyrus said.

"And let us get back home," Casey added.

Luis never liked the game where you set up dominoes and when you pushed one, they all began to fall. It looked easier than it really was. He had a feeling if they weren't careful, the dominoes would fall the wrong way and then everything would stop.

Luis took a deep breath. "So, first we have to find the money. Then all we have to do is get the police to capture the thieves and rescue the camera crew."

He let out a big sigh.

Tyler jumped up. "I have an idea of how to find that money. But if it goes wrong, we might be captured too."

Luis looked at Tyler, Casey, and Steel.

If they were all captured, who would rescue them?

THE MONEY!

Tyler walked around the room. He tapped the wall with his crutch. He tapped the floor. He tapped the corners and the door.

"Thomas, when you were chasing those gangsters, do you remember what room you saw them in last?" Tyler asked. "Sometimes when I'm building a robot part, I have to be like a detective and think about what happens next. Right now, we need to think about what happened before."

The ghost nodded. He gave a big sigh. "Yes, it was the room where I had my accident and died."

"Accident?" Luis asked. "You weren't killed by the gangsters?"

"No. Everyone thought I was, but I had no way of telling them differently," Thomas said. "Come with me."

Thomas drifted down the hallway and to the big stairs that led to the main floor. Luis and his friends followed him.

Luis had an idea what Tyler's plan was for finding the money. But after all these years, maybe it had been found and taken away. Maybe Thomas couldn't remember where he'd been last. And maybe that wasn't where the gangsters hid the money.

"If we find the money, what will we do next?" Luis said, picking up Steel to carry it downstairs.

"Get out of here and find the police," Tyler said.

Uncle Cyrus's voice said, "I wish I could make this thing move faster. Using it as a radio isn't good enough. Did I hear you say you were going to leave this house to get the police? Isn't that dangerous? We don't know what would happen if I can't return us to the Time Twister."

Luis followed the ghost through a large library with a few dusty books on shelves and into the kitchen. The kitchen looked as if someone had taken a hammer to it. A lot of hammers.

Thomas stopped. Luis kept moving and walked right through the ghost. He shivered.

"Ugh, it's like walking through a freezer," Luis said, setting down Steel.

Thomas stood in the center of the large kitchen. "It was above my head," he said.

Casey looked up. There was nothing above them but a cracked ceiling, broken tiles, and a big hole.

"What? The hole?" she said.

"There was a large, heavy light there. The owners of the house had everything brought from around the world. Fancy tile, special woodwork, enormous books. This light was made of solid iron. But they didn't make sure it was hung properly," Thomas said.

Luis gasped. "You mean it fell on you?"

"Yes. I had cornered the two gangsters. They were about to leave when I found them," Thomas said. Suddenly his ghostly body was less see-through. His uniform looked new. His hat tilted on his head.

Luis backed away. There were two men standing near a large cupboard in the wall. They wore dark suits and had angry expressions.

"You shouldn't have followed us here, copper!" one yelled.

Thomas pointed his hand at them, as if he had once carried a weapon. "Give up, boys! There are more police on the way! Where's the loot?"

One of the men laughed. It was loud and sounded like a donkey's bray. "We aren't telling you anything."

Suddenly, the other man looked up. His mouth fell open, just as a large chandelier dropped from the ceiling.

Casey screamed as it fell toward Thomas.

Then the men were gone. Thomas was once again a see-through figure.

He pointed to the cupboard where the men had been standing. "They were bending down inside that cupboard when I walked in," Thomas said.

Luis and Casey ran to the cupboard. Tyler and Steel followed them.

Luis ripped and tugged until he pulled away the cupboard doors. He crawled into the opening, realizing the cupboard was very deep. After a moment of feeling around in the dark, he shouted, "Give me a flashlight!"

Casey put a flashlight in his hand. He shone it around. He could tell someone had been digging in there before. The sides had large holes all

CRASH!

around. After sixty years, how could the money still be there?

He reached his free hand inside each of the holes. Something crawled over his hand and he yanked it out. He closed his eyes and took a deep breath.

"Where did those guys put that money?" he said under his breath.

"Did you find anything?" Casey shouted.

"No!" Luis said. "And stop yelling. Those thieves upstairs could be downstairs by now, you know."

Luis crawled across the floor inside the cupboard. The wood creaked under his knee. He shone the flashlight on the spot.

"That's it!" he said. Luis tapped the flashlight on the floorboards. There was an echo with two of them.

He said, "Casey, I need some kind of thin tool to pry up a board."

He heard Casey's jacket clanking, then the sound of a zipper. Her hand reached into the cupboard, holding out a tool that looked like a butter knife with a flat hook on the end.

Luis worked the hook in between the creaky floorboards and pulled. With a crack, the old wood pulled away. When he had pulled up two boards, he reached inside.

"I feel something," he said. He grabbed at a piece of cloth and pulled. In his hand was a bag with the faded word *FLOUR* on it. A rope had been wrapped around the top of the bag.

Luis set down the flashlight so it stood on the floor. Then he opened the bag.

"Wow!" he said. "It's *full* of money. Lots of money. Old money!"

He crawled to the opening of the cupboard and back into the light.

"Hey, did you hear what I said? I found the money," Luis said.

"That's great, kid. Now hand it over," a gruff voice said.

Luis looked up to see the bearded guy holding out a gloved hand. The other thief was holding Casey and Tyler by their arms.

"Just stand up slow and drop your weapon," the bearded man said.

Luis dropped the tool and stood. The man grabbed the bag from Luis's hand.

"You sure saved us a lot of trouble," the other man said. "You must be with those other people we nabbed."

Luis shouted, "Thomas! We need your help!"

The bearded man whirled around. "You've got someone else helping you?" Then he snarled, "We'll get him, too."

Luis shook his head. "He went for the police. They'll be here any minute."

The man holding Casey and Tyler laughed. "We will be long gone by then. With the money."

The bearded man nodded and laughed. But when he looked at his friend, his eyes opened wide and he stopped laughing. He pointed behind the other man.

"What's wrong? You look like you seen a ghost," the other thief said. He turned his head and yelled. He let go of Tyler's arm and shoved Casey toward the floating figure of Thomas.

"It *is* a ghost!" the bearded thief yelled. "A police ghost!"

Thomas moved toward them. He pointed to the badge on his shirt. His voice echoed around the room. "You are under arrest for trespassing, kidnapping, vandalism, and stealing! Hands up! Now, I say!"

The bearded man fell to his knees. "Don't make us ghosts! We weren't going to hurt them. Here, the money is yours." He threw the bag toward Thomas and jumped up.

Luis grabbed the bag and tossed it to Casey.

Thomas floated in front of the door to the kitchen. The thieves huddled on the floor and hid their faces.

"Quick, find rope and tie their hands," Tyler said.

Casey grinned. "A girl never knows when she might need rope." She reached inside her jacket and pulled out a thick piece of rope.

Luis grabbed it. "Gosh, Casey, is there anything you don't have inside that coat?"

He told the thieves to hold out their hands and then wrapped the rope around them as Thomas hovered above the scene.

"We'll cooperate," the bearded man said. "Just keep that ghost cop away from us!"

Casey turned to Thomas. "What do we do next? How do we help you?"

Thomas said, "I don't know. But you can help your friends upstairs. And, you need to bring the police here. The station is only a block away."

Casey nodded. She said, "I'll be right back."

Luis watched her hurry from the kitchen. He heard the front door open and close.

"This was easy," he said. "We'll be on our way home soon."

Steel rolled into the kitchen.

Tyler called his robot cat to his side. "Hey, where have you been?"

Uncle Cyrus's voice said, "This cat has been wandering around the house. I tried to make it stop, but it doesn't listen to my commands. It moved in circles around a table in the library, making that miserable meowing noise."

Luis said, "He must need a repair. But what matters is that we've captured the thieves and Casey is returning the money and bringing the police. They can help the crew upstairs and we can go. Right?"

Cyrus said, "Perhaps. Yet I do not feel that this is why I am here."

Tyler groaned. "What? You mean we captured crooks, met a ghost, found money that had been missing for decades, and we're still stuck here?"

"Yes, I am afraid we are stuck in this house," Uncle Cyrus said. "You must help me find why I have been brought here, or we cannot leave."

UP THE RAMP

Luis paced the kitchen. He glared at the men tied up on the floor.

Finally, he picked up Steel and put him on the stained kitchen counter. "Why do you think you aren't done here, Uncle Cyrus?"

"It's hard to explain. When we left the spaceship, I could feel things shifting. I was no longer able to see the ship or feel a part of it. But here, I have no problem communicating with you and your friends. And, more important, I saw Tesla. Upstairs. In the attic when I followed the thieves and your camera people."

Tyler walked over to the counter. He stared into Steel's face. "What? You saw Tesla? Is his ghost here, too?"

"Not his ghost. But his presence is here. I believe he has been trying to locate me since the day he discovered I was missing," Cyrus said.

"That's just too weird," Tyler said.

Luis put his hand on Tyler's arm. "Can you watch these guys by yourself until the police come? I'm going to go set the crew free and see if I can find out what Uncle Cyrus is talking about."

Thomas appeared beside them, sitting on the counter. "He will not be alone. I will make sure these crooks do not leave before the police arrive to take them away."

The bearded thief trembled at the sight of Thomas. "We *want* them to take us away from here. We're ready to go."

Luis picked up Casey's hooked tool from the floor and put it in his pocket so it wouldn't get left behind. He grabbed Steel and walked upstairs. Then he moved toward the attic ladder.

"Go into the room where the camera crew disappeared," Uncle Cyrus said. "There is a secret panel there that hides a ramp that goes up to the attic. There will be no need to climb those steps while carrying the cat."

Luis looked down the long hallway full of doors. He headed straight for the first room the camera crew had gone into.

Uncle Cyrus said, "When the hidden door opened, there was a series of knocks on the wall from the inside. Three quick taps, silence, then two more, silence, then one last tap. The cameraman was shouting for you to come inside. I believe they thought it was the ghost hitting the wall."

Luis set down Steel, went to the corner wall, and hit it three times with his fist. He waited a moment, hit it twice more, and waited again.

"Here goes," he said.

Luis hit the wall once more.

The wall swung away, revealing the ramp. Luis grinned. "That is pretty amazing for such an old house."

Steel rolled behind him. "I suspect that wall was added later by other owners."

At the top of the ramp, Luis hurried across the hall to the room where he'd seen the robbers and the crew before.

Bob, Parker, and Darla were still sitting on the floor, their hands and feet tied. Luis ran inside and began untying the ropes. He took the cloths from around their mouths.

"What's going on?" Bob asked. "Where are those men? They are thieves who are looking for the lost bank money."

"We know," Luis said. He undid the last of the ropes on Darla's ankles.

The crew stood, stretching sore limbs.

"The men are tied up in the kitchen," Luis said.

Parker's eyes went wide. "You three captured them?"

Darla rubbed her arms. "They took our equipment. They pushed us around. Terrifying."

Luis said, "We found something even more terrifying."

Darla laughed and asked, "What? A ghost?"

Luis nodded.

"For real?" Bob said. "Where is it? Let's talk to it. Is the ghost angry or looking for revenge or just plain bad?"

"None of those things," Luis said. "Go downstairs and wait for the police. Tell them about the men kidnapping the three of you. Tyler will explain everything about Thomas, the ghost. I have to look for something up here."

After they left, Luis put Steel on the ground. "Did Tesla say anything to you?"

Steel rolled across the room, its metal tail moving back and forth.

"Where are you going?" Luis asked.

Uncle Cyrus shouted, "I am not going anywhere. This metal creature goes where it wants. I can only see, hear, and speak through it. I cannot yet control its movements."

The robot stopped when it ran into a wall.

Uncle Cyrus moaned. "As I was about to say, Tesla did not speak. At least, I could not hear what he was saying. He mouthed words at me. He pointed to that dresser against the wall. Then, he faded and disappeared."

Luis walked over to the dresser. It had three large drawers and two smaller ones. One of the smaller drawers had a lock on it.

Luis yanked open each of the other drawers. He felt all around inside. Then he pulled them out one by one and looked behind them.

Uncle Cyrus was yelling at Steel to turn around. After several moments, the cat sat down and stared at the wall.

"Ridiculous creature!" Cyrus said. "Luis, have you looked in all of the drawers?"

Luis looked at the stack of drawers on the floor. "All of them except for one. It's locked."

Cyrus said, "Find something to pick the lock."

Luis walked around the room. There was not much left in the old house after so many years.

He folded his arms. If he had a hammer, he could break open the drawer. Or a long pick to stick into the lock. "Oh, wow, what's the matter with me?" Luis said. He reached into his pocket for Casey's tool. "This should do it."

Luis worked the curved end of the tool into the top edge of the drawer. It slid inside. He turned the tool slightly and pulled. The drawer's front broke away.

He felt around in the drawer. "Nothing."

Luis ran over to Steel and turned the cat away from the wall. Immediately it moved back to face the wall.

Luis said, "Listen, I'll be back. As soon as Casey comes back with the police and those crooks are gone, we'll come back up here. Wait here in case you see Tesla again."

Luis hurried out the door and down the ramp, through the secret panel in the wall, and into the large room.

He walked toward the door to the hall. It slammed shut. The air in the room turned cold and Luis shivered.

"Okay, Thomas. What's the big idea?" Luis shouted.

Two wispy figures appeared in front of the door.

"Get out!" one yelled. "And take that ghost of a copper with you!"

The other one brayed with laughter.

The door swung open and Luis flew through it. As he ran down the stairs, he could hear laughter echoing all around him.

He ran into the front room as a policeman led the robbers out the door and into his car.

Casey and Tyler stood at the kitchen door.

"Hey, what's all the noise?" Tyler asked.

Luis waved his arms and pointed upstairs. "Ghosts! There are two more ghosts up there!"

Thomas appeared in front of Luis. "I thought they were gone for good."

Casey said, "Who?"

Thomas frowned. "Those are the gangsters who robbed the bank. They must be here for the money since you found it, Luis."

Luis looked up the stairs. The two ghosts were leaning over the railing.

Howling like the wind, they leaped over the railing and came straight toward Luis.

THE SHANNON BROTHERS

Luis ran. "Thomas!"

The ghostly gangsters yelled, "Where's our money?"

They swirled around Luis and his friends. The camera crew ran in from the kitchen.

"Wow! Supernatural manifestations!" Bob shouted. He held up the video camera. "Parker! Record those voices!"

Parker grabbed for the recorder. One of the gangsters moved in front of him and the machine flew into the air.

Darla held up an infrared thermometer to record the temperature of the spirits.

"That dame is pointing one of those machines at us!" the donkey-laughing ghost shouted.

The thermometer whipped out of Darla's hand. Soon, all the ghost-hunting machines were swirling around them.

"Give us our money and leave!" one of the ghostly gangsters shouted. His fedora sat crooked over one eye. His suit jacket flapped behind him.

"What'll we do?" Tyler asked. He waved his crutch in the air. The ghosts whirled around it, then yanked it into the air to float with the camera crew's equipment.

"Leave, my friends," Thomas called over the noise. "This is between me and the Shannon brothers."

"We can't go," Casey said. "Luis's uncle Cyrus brought us here. We're stuck until we see this through."

The real police hadn't taken the money yet. So Casey grabbed the bag and held it up for everyone to see.

"This isn't your money, you crooks. But if you want it, come and get it!" She stood still as the ghosts moved toward her.

"Over here!" Luis shouted. He held out his hands and caught the bag when Casey tossed it.

"That money is ours!" the gangsters sneered.

Luis threw the bag back to Casey. She ran past Tyler, who reached out with his free hand and took it from her.

Tyler ducked and clutched the money bag as the ghosts swooped down at him. They reached for the bag as he turned away from them.

Luis ran across the room. He grabbed Tyler's floating crutch and swung it around.

"You can't hit them!" Thomas said.

Luis grinned. "Ever play baseball, Thomas?"

Thomas raised an eyebrow.

Luis swung the crutch at the bag of money in Tyler's hand. As Tyler let go, the crutch hit it and sent the bag flying across the room.

Thomas floated straight up and stopped the bag in front of him. It floated above his hands.

"This money doesn't belong to you crooks. I am taking it and we are leaving this place to the living."

Thomas extended his ghostly hand toward the money. The gangsters whirled toward him.

"Watch out!" Luis shouted.

Thomas flipped over the bag of money and grabbed it from behind. The gangsters yelled. Their wispy bodies seemed to squish and fold.

Thomas opened the bag and the gangsters slipped inside.

"Great job," Casey said.

Thomas took off his hat and bowed. "Thank you, Miss Casey."

His body became even more transparent. "It's time for me to leave this house. I've captured my gangsters and, thanks to you three, I have reclaimed the money that they stole."

And he was gone.

The camera crew shouted and hugged one another. "We did it! Our first real ghost sighting!"

Bob came over and shook Luis's hand. "No one will accuse you of being fakers ever again."

Luis grinned. He'd never dreamed of having an adventure in a real haunted house. He promised himself to thank Uncle Cyrus for bringing them there.

"Uncle Cyrus!" Luis yelled. "I left him upstairs and told him I'd be right back."

Casey and Tyler hurried upstairs behind Luis, leaving the others behind.

"There's a secret way to get into the attic," Luis said. He showed them the open wall and the ramp that led to the attic.

He ran into the room where the thieves had kept the camera crew. Steel stood in the same place, its cold nose against the wall beside the dresser.

"Oh, sorry, Uncle Cyrus, I didn't mean to take so long," Luis said. "But wait until you hear what happened."

Casey pulled Steel away from the wall. It rolled back to the wall until its nose touched it again.

Tyler laughed.

"Your cat is so weird," Casey said. She picked up the cat and held it in the air. Steel's wheeled feet moved as if it were rolling back to the wall.

Luis touched the cat's back. "Hey, Uncle Cyrus. Are you angry? Don't you want to hear what happened? There were other ghosts here. The two gangsters who stole the money and caused Thomas to die came after us."

Steel was silent.

"Uncle Cyrus?" Luis asked.

Casey put the cat back onto the floor. They watched as it rolled to the wall until it bumped against it once again.

"I think Cyrus is gone," Casey whispered.

Luis picked up Steel and stared into the robot's face. "He can't be gone. We're still here."

"He left us behind?" Tyler asked. "After tricking us into coming here? We helped solve the mystery. We helped the ghosts leave this house. And we helped the Haunting Exterminators prove they could do the job. So, why aren't we headed home?"

Luis looked at the wall in front of him. He put Steel back on the floor. The cat rolled straight to the wall, its feet still moving when it was against the wall.

"Uncle Cyrus said he saw Tesla by this dresser. Cyrus thought Tesla was trying to tell him something. I thought it was something about the dresser, but maybe not," Luis said.

He banged his hand on the wall.

"I think there's something behind here we need to find."

Casey reached into her coat and unzipped a tall pocket. She pulled out a thin piece of metal. She pressed a button and it began to grow longer. When it stopped, the top flipped open to reveal a small silver crowbar.

"Wow, that's the littlest crowbar I've ever seen," Luis said. "I don't think it'll do much good."

Casey walked to the wall.

"Watch out," Tyler said.

She swung the crowbar against the wall. It broke a small hole into the wall. Then, like a spider web, cracks moved out from the hole until a large part of the wall began to crumble.

"Wow!" Luis said.

Tyler said, "She and my father built that. It's stronger than any steel used for normal tools. It's like something a superhero would carry."

Luis held his breath as he walked over to the wall.

A Clue in Time

Luis peeked into the dark hole. He reached in and moved his hand down as far as he could. It was the second hole he'd dug around in that day. Hopefully nothing wriggly lived in this one.

"The next hole in the wall or floor we find, one of you gets to stick your hand in it," Luis said.

He stretched and wiggled his fingers. He felt something.

"There's something there. It's just out of my reach," Luis said. "It's some kind of paper."

Casey nudged his arm. "My arms are longer than yours. Let me try."

Luis moved away and Casey took his place. He watched her bend down into the wall.

"Nope, can't reach it either," she said.

Luis groaned. "Can't we just break more of the wall farther down?"

Casey slapped her palm against her forehead. "Of course. What kind of adventurers are we?"

She kicked at the wall below the hole. Luis kicked with her. The wall near the floor started to break apart.

"Move aside, amateurs," Tyler said.

He leaned against one crutch and swung the other hard against the wall. The old plaster gave way.

Luis knelt down beside the hole and looked inside. He could see a piece of paper wrapped around a box.

"Eureka!" he yelled.

Casey grabbed it from his hand. "It looks like it's been here a long time. The paper is all yellow and crinkly."

"Be careful with it. We don't want it to fall apart before we read it," Tyler said.

Casey slowly unfolded the paper around the box. She gave the paper to Luis.

He opened it and read. "My dear friend Cyrus, it has been weeks and you have not returned. I fear that you are trapped in the machine's pull on time. Why did you try this alone? You are much too curious a fellow. I have tried reprogramming the Time Twister, but nothing seems to work.

"I fear an attempt to follow you and bring you home. If I were to disappear, there would be no one to rescue us, as there is no one else who understands this machine. I will keep a journal of my efforts. Hoping we will soon be together again. Yours, Nikola."

"Wow," Tyler said. "He was a great friend."

"Too bad he never got Uncle Cyrus home," Luis said.

Casey shook her head. "But don't you see? If time isn't a straight line, somewhere in the past, Tesla is still trying to find your uncle. It had to be years later that he left this in the wall. And how did your uncle see him today?"

Luis grinned. Time travel made his head spin. But if Casey was right, then they weren't the only ones trying to help Uncle Cyrus.

"What's in the box?" Tyler asked.

Luis held it up. It was a small copper box with a hinged lid. He opened it.

"What's that?" Casey asked.

Luis pulled out a long silver chain with a round silver watch attached to it.

"It's an old pocket watch!" Casey said. She touched the face of the watch. "I've taken apart a bunch of these. This one is nice."

Luis removed a small piece of paper from inside the box.

"It's another note from Tesla," he said. He read the note out loud. "Cyrus, I found your watch outside the Time Twister. You must have dropped it. This watch, having belonged to your father, is perhaps a link to you and your time. I am hiding it in the wall of this house where I am staying. Should your time travel bring you here, it might anchor your time line again. Nikola."

Luis turned the watch over.

"There's writing on the back," he said.

Tyler leaned in and read. "Time never stops. It always waits to change our lives."

Luis stuffed the note and the watch back into the box, then wrapped the letter around it and put them in his pocket.

"Uncle Cyrus needs to see this. This was why he needed us here."

Luis felt the pull of the Time Twister. He closed his eyes again so he wouldn't see his friends twisting and fading away.

All around him was wind and strange movement as they headed home.

This time, he wasn't leaving the Time Twister until he tried to contact Uncle Cyrus. He had important information.

FADE IN, FADE OUT

"We're back home, Luis," Casey said.

Luis took a deep breath. He opened his eyes. They were back in Tesla's Time Twister. Everything looked the same as before.

Everything except the hologram head of his uncle Cyrus sitting on the control panel staring out at Luis.

"Welcome back," the head said.

Luis tried to talk, but nothing came out of his mouth except a little squeaking noise.

"Take deep breaths," Uncle Cyrus said. "It's not my real head. It's a projection. I've been working while waiting for the three of you. With the Time Twister being used again, I'm finding that I can do more and more."

Luis jumped out of his seat. "You've been working? We were stuck back there all alone. How can you be working?"

Tyler walked up to the hologram. He moved his hand through it. "There's energy here. It's not like with Thomas. This is science, not something supernatural."

Luis pointed to Steel. "Does this mean you won't be talking through Steel anymore?"

"No, I will still need the robot cat to communicate when we are in other times and places, but here, I can speak to you in this form," Cyrus said.

Casey waved her hand in front of Cyrus's head. "Are you saying you want us to do this again? Sorry, but I've had it. I'd rather be learning something new in the safety of my garage than on one of Luis's wild adventures."

Luis glared at her. "It wasn't my idea to break into the shed and find this thing." He stuck his hands in his pockets. He touched the letter and watch box. "Hey, wait! We found something at that old house. It was from Tesla."

Uncle Cyrus's mouth opened wide. "Show it to me!"

Luis pulled out the box wrapped with Tesla's letter. He read the letter out loud again.

"My good friend! He did not give up on me. And in his time, he is still searching for a way to bring me home," Cyrus said. His holographic head shimmered.

"We also found this," Luis said. He opened the box and took out the watch.

"My watch!" Cyrus shouted. "I have missed it. I always had it with me."

"I don't think it's working," Luis said. He shook the watch.

"Wind it, please," Uncle Cyrus said.

Casey took it from Luis's hand and wound it.

"Nope, it doesn't move at all," she said.

She turned it over. Quickly, she reached into her jacket and pulled out her tiny toolbox.

"What is she doing to my watch?" Cyrus asked. His voice rose in a panic.

Casey pried off the back of the watch. "I'm going to see if I can repair it," she said.

She pulled out a small round object from another pocket and put it over her eye.

"What's that?" Luis asked.

"It's a jeweler's loupe," Casey said. "It's like a magnifying glass."

She held the open watch in the palm of her hand. She bent over it to work. Casey hummed as she took a tiny screwdriver and poked around the gears of the watch.

"Yes, there's a little loose pin. I just need to slide it back into place." She grunted, then looked up. "Done!"

In a moment, she had replaced the back cover.

Luis took the watch and held it up. "It's working now, Uncle Cyrus."

He showed the ticking watch to his uncle's hologram. Cyrus grinned.

Then, his head disappeared.

"Hey, what happened?" Tyler asked.

Luis shouted, "Uncle Cyrus, where are you? Are you all right?"

There was nothing but silence.

Luis ran around the Time Twister. He peeked into corners and behind the control panel.

"Look!" Casey said. She pointed to the fourth seat, where Uncle Cyrus sat.

Uncle Cyrus smiled at them. "Hello nephew and friends."

Luis thought his mouth would drop to the floor. "Uncle Cyrus! Are you real?"

His uncle stood and picked up the old watch. He stuck it in his pocket and patted it.

"I have always been real, my boy. Just not in your time," Cyrus said.

"Are you real in this time now?" Casey asked. She stepped forward, reached out, and touched his arm. "You feel real," she said.

Cyrus put a hand on Luis's shoulder. "Thank you for going to the old house. And for bringing back the things that Tesla left for me."

He took a deep breath. "It feels different from how I feel when I'm a prisoner of this tiresome machine. I will hate to return to that state, but I know this cannot last. Not yet."

Luis said, "Return? But, aren't you here for good? I know it's not your time, but you'll love it staying with us."

Suddenly, the Time Twister began to shake. Steam came out of every dial on the control panel.

"What's happening?" Tyler yelled. He reached a foot out to steady Steel, who was tilting sideways.

"This isn't my time and it is disrupting yours," Uncle Cyrus said. "Take the watch. Keep it with you until Tesla sends me further clues on how to return. If there are further clues. If I can't return to my time, I must stay a part of Tesla's machine."

Cyrus took the watch from his pocket and put it into Luis's hands. As he did, his body began to fade.

"I will speak to you again through the cat this time tomorrow," Cyrus said. "I need to understand what the Time Twister wants us to do next."

Casey asked, "Us?"

"Next?" Tyler said.

Cyrus nodded and disappeared.

The Time Twister stopped shaking. Steel rolled to the door of the machine. The door slid open, and the cat moved toward the stairs.

Luis looked at his friends. "So, that was an exciting trip, wasn't it?"

Casey pulled her jacket tighter. It rattled and clanked. "We visited a creepy old house, got captured by thieves, were attacked by gangster ghosts, and wound up saved by a ghost cop. That might be a little *too* much excitement."

Luis shrugged. "Yeah, but we're home now. And who else could say they had a spring break like this one? It's our secret."

They stepped out of Tesla's Time Twister and back into the shed.

Luis hurried toward the door. Tyler moved ahead of him and barred the door with a crutch.

"Your uncle Cyrus said he'd talk with us again tomorrow. Did you forget our dads will be back soon? If they aren't already," Tyler said.

Luis pointed to the clock on the wall. "Look at the time. We've only been gone a couple of minutes. We aren't leaving anything behind to show we've been in here. We have to come back tomorrow and find out if Tesla has tried contacting Uncle Cyrus again."

Luis pushed Tyler's crutch away and walked outside. When everyone was standing outside the shed, he put the strange lock back on and stuck the key in his pocket next to Cyrus's watch.

He grabbed Steel and stalked across the yard to his back porch. He put Steel on top of the picnic table and sat in front of the robot cat.

"Boy, Uncle Cyrus, you're getting me into a pile of trouble with my best friends and maybe our dads, too, if they find out what we've done. I just don't know what to do."

Steel opened its mouth.

MEOWWRR! BOING!

"You said it," Luis said.

Casey and Tyler joined him at the table. Tyler grabbed Steel and turned him over. He unscrewed a section of the cat's back and began poking at a tiny keypad.

Luis grabbed Tyler's arm and yelled, "Hey, are you turning him off so Uncle Cyrus can't talk through him?"

Tyler shook Luis's hand away. "No! Let go. I'm just trying to fix his meow."

Casey leaned forward. "This has been so exciting. Space, a giant robot, aliens, weird ghost detecting machines. I've never learned so much in just a few minutes."

Luis nodded. "Exactly. Hard to believe it's just a few minutes of our real time."

"As long we don't get stuck like your uncle," Tyler said. He closed Steel's panel and pressed a button under the cat's chin.

"Okay, I think I've fixed it," Tyler said.

They leaned closer to Steel. Its eyes flashed. Its tail whirled. It opened its mouth.

BOWWOW!

Luis laughed. He put his hand on Tyler's arm. Casey grinned and put a hand on Luis's shoulder.

"We're not the Three Musketeers," Luis said. "But we're the Three Time Twisters."

The three friends all smiled and nodded.

"We'll find a way to keep our dads away tomorrow. And we'll see what adventure Uncle Cyrus has for us next in Tesla's Time Twister," Luis said.

Luis went inside to get some snacks. They would need a planning session for whatever might happen next.

He pulled out the watch and read. "Time never stops. It always waits to change our lives."

He had no idea where time would take them next. But he did know their lives would be changed, no matter where, or *when*, they went.

Luis grabbed three bottles of juice and his dad's giant jar of trail mix. Then he picked up the Monopoly game off the kitchen counter.

You can always learn something in an adventurous game of Monopoly, he thought as he ran out to the backyard.

He looked at the shed just beyond the yard.

"Don't worry, Uncle Cyrus," he said. "We won't give up."

For a moment, something in the shed seemed to hum. Then, it was quiet.

Luis tossed the game onto the table. For now, a game with his best friends was the only adventure he wanted.